For Suleiman, Josè, Naima, Dagma, Flavia, Brunilda, Hagar, Jo, Hasna and all the others who had to leave their first homes and were brave enough to find new ones – M.H.

For Christina – K.L.

**ARABIC WORDS**

*qu'ran* **(Koran)**
The sacred book of Islam, believed by Moslems to be the word of God revealed to Mohammed

*hajab*
Traditional head covering worn by Moslem women

*The Colour of Home* copyright © Frances Lincoln Limited 2002
Text copyright © Mary Hoffman 2002
Illustrations copyright © Karin Littlewood 2002

First published in Great Britain in 2002 by
Frances Lincoln Limited, 4 Torriano Mews
Torriano Avenue, London NW5 2RZ

www.franceslincoln.com

With thanks for help to Jill Rutter, formerly of the Refugee Council; Sandi Santos, formerly
of Homeless Action in Barnet; Sahra Haid at the Tawakal Somali Women's Group in Limehouse;
and Laila Jama at the Haringey Somali Community Association

British Library Cataloguing in Publication Data available on request

ISBN 0-7112-1940-0

Set in Cochin

Printed in Singapore

3 5 7 9 8 6 4 2

# The Colour
# of Home

## Mary Hoffman
## Illustrated by Karin Littlewood

FRANCES LINCOLN

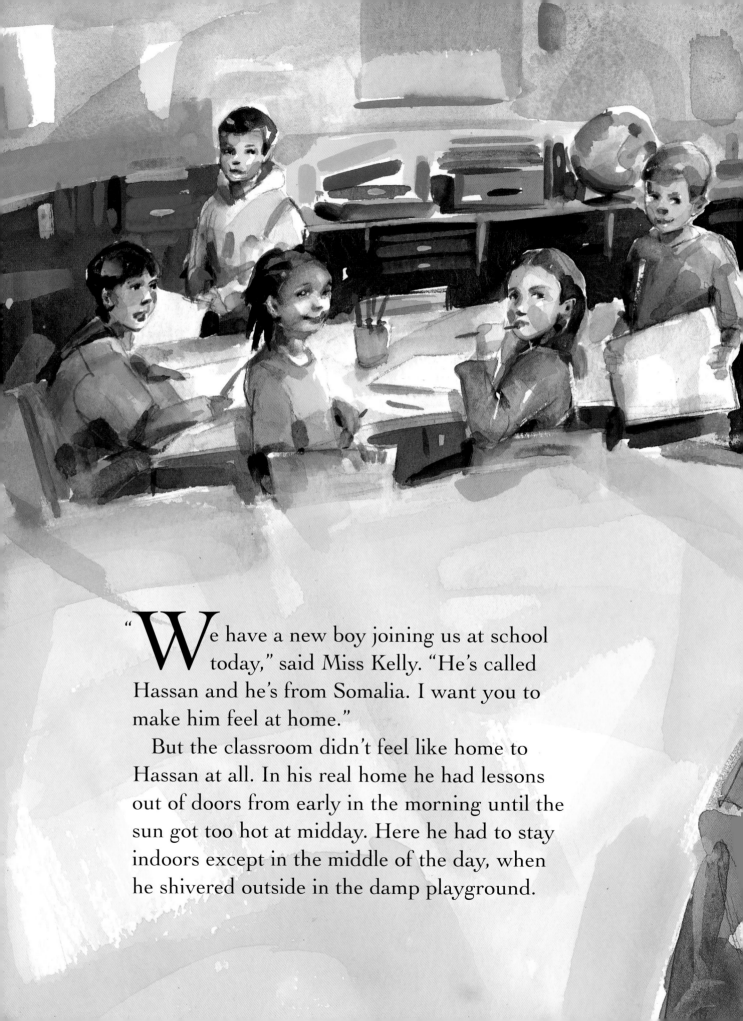

"We have a new boy joining us at school today," said Miss Kelly. "He's called Hassan and he's from Somalia. I want you to make him feel at home."

But the classroom didn't feel like home to Hassan at all. In his real home he had lessons out of doors from early in the morning until the sun got too hot at midday. Here he had to stay indoors except in the middle of the day, when he shivered outside in the damp playground.

The children were friendly. They smiled
at Hassan and one of the boys kicked
a football towards him. But he didn't
understand anything that anyone said –
only his name and "hello" and "toilet".
It was tiring remembering even a few
English words.

After lunch, which Hassan didn't eat, because he didn't know what it was, Miss Kelly gave all the children big sheets of gritty grey paper and pinned them to easels. She gave Hassan paintbrushes and a pot of water and showed him where all the colours were. He understood from her smiles and movements that she wanted him to paint a picture, but he had never done such a thing before.

He watched the other children for a while, then chose a bottle of bright blue.

He painted a blue, blue sky, without any clouds. Then a white
house, a yellow sun and mimosa trees. Outside the house
he made stick figures – himself, his father, his mother holding
a bundle that was his baby sister, his grandparents, his uncle,
his two cousins. There were nine people outside the house,
who all lived inside it.

Then Hassan took more paint and put in the animals –
a flock of white sheep, some brown goats and a small
sandy creature who was supposed to be his cat.

"What a lovely picture, Hassan," said Miss Kelly.
"What beautiful bright colours!"

But Hassan hadn't finished. Now he chose red and orange and painted big flames on the roof of the house. The blue sky changed to a murky purple. He drew another stick figure with a gun, and made black bullets come out of it. He took the red paint again and splattered it on the white walls of the house. He smudged his uncle out of the picture.

"Oh, Hassan," said Miss Kelly. "It's all spoilt. What a shame!"
Hassan didn't know what her words meant, but he heard the
sadness in her voice and knew that she understood his picture.

"What did you do at school today?" asked his mother, when she brought his little sister Naima to collect him.

"Painting," said Hassan.

"Can I see?" she said. All around them, other children were showing their pictures to their mothers.

"No," said Hassan. "The paint is still wet." He didn't want his mother to be sad. "You can see it tomorrow."

The next day, Hassan wanted to tell
Miss Kelly that he must make a new
picture. But she had someone
with her, a Somali lady
wearing a black *hajab* like
his mother's – only she also
wore blue jeans and a black
leather jacket, like a
Western woman.

"Hello, Hassan," said the woman. Then she began to speak to him in Somali. "I'm Fela, I've come to translate for you and help with your English. Miss Kelly thought you might want to tell us about your picture."

So another teacher taught the rest of the class maths, and Hassan sat in the reading corner with Fela and Miss Kelly and his picture.

"That's my house in Somalia," he said, looking at Fela, who put his words into English. "That's my family." And he named them all, right down to the baby. "And that's my cat, Musa, who we had to leave behind."

"And who is this?" asked Miss Kelly, pointing to the smudge near the red splashes.

"That's my uncle Ahmed," said Hassan. And then he told them the whole story – about the noise, the flames, the bullets and the awful smell of burning and blood.

"When the soldiers came, I hid in my
cousins' room," he said. "I didn't find out what
happened to my uncle until later. My father came and fetched
me out from under the bed and said we were leaving.

"We all went straight away, except my uncle. We had no luggage, only my father's prayer mat and *qu'ran*, hidden in Naima's bag of nappies. I wanted to take Musa, my cat, but my mother said we must save ourselves and not the animals. I cried then, not for my uncle, but for Musa.

"We went on a big ship from Mogadishu to Mombasa. Then we lived in a camp for a long time. Naima learned to walk there. It was cold at night and my mother had to queue for our food. People stole things and all my mother's gold jewellery disappeared, but I think that was because we bought tickets to England. My cousins and grandparents stayed behind.

I was frightened when I saw the plane we were going to fly in, because I thought it might have bombs in it. The journey was so long, but I wasn't happy when it was over. Our new country seemed all cold and grey. And the flat we live in is grey too, with brown furniture. We seem to have left all the colours behind in Somalia."

Hassan talked for an hour and then he ran out of words, even in Somali. When he finished, Miss Kelly had tears in her eyes.

"Tell her I want to make another picture," Hassan said to Fela, "for my mother."

Then he played football with the friendly boy, who pointed to himself and said, "Jake".

That afternoon, Hassan painted a new picture. It had blue sky, the white house and the yellow mimosa. But this time there were no people – just sheep and goats and Musa the cat with his long spindly legs. There were no flames or bullets. By going-home time the picture was dry.

"It's beautiful," said
Hassan's mother.
"It's our home in Somalia,"
said Hassan.
"I know," said his mother.
"We'll put it on the wall of
our home here in England."
"Let me push Naima,"
said Hassan, and he walked
home pushing his little sister
in her pushchair.

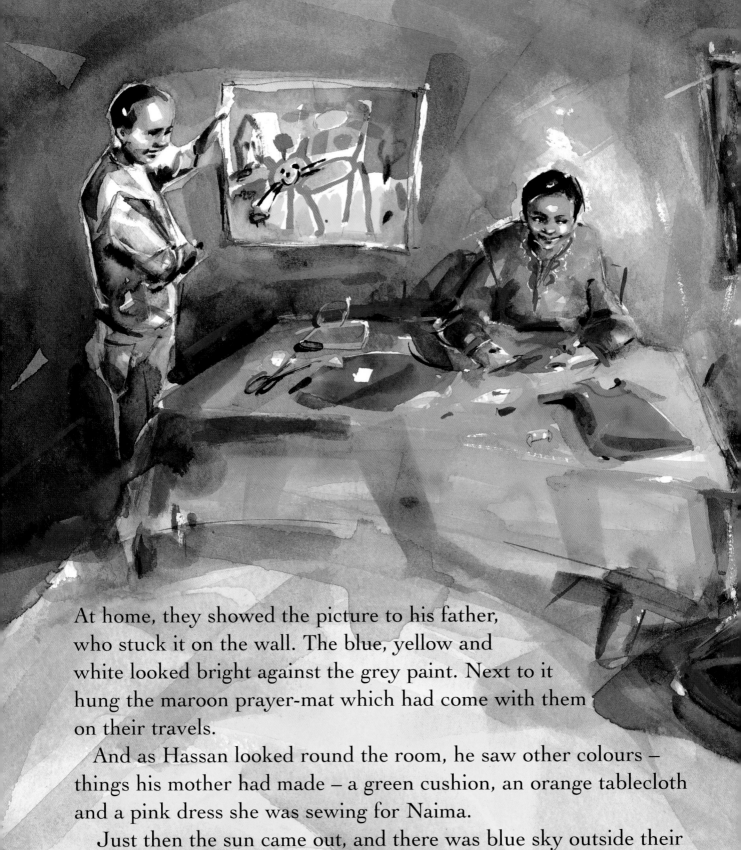

At home, they showed the picture to his father,
who stuck it on the wall. The blue, yellow and
white looked bright against the grey paint. Next to it
hung the maroon prayer-mat which had come with them
on their travels.

And as Hassan looked round the room, he saw other colours –
things his mother had made – a green cushion, an orange tablecloth
and a pink dress she was sewing for Naima.

Just then the sun came out, and there was blue sky outside their
window. Hassan looked at his family and said, "Daddy, can we have
a new cat?" and he said "cat" in English. It was one of the new words
he had learned today.

Tomorrow he would ask Miss Kelly to tell him the word for "home".